Steck-Vaughn
POINT of **VIEW** **Stories**

Grow Up, Peter Pan!

By
Dr. Alvin Granowsky

Illustrated by
Stephen Marchesi

RSVP
RAINTREE
STECK-VAUGHN
PUBLISHERS
The Steck-Vaughn Company

Austin, Texas

Shhhh! Not a peep from you! The word's out that I was dinner for a croc. And that's the way we must keep it for now.

Now don't scream because I have some scars on my face. I'm not out to harm you, mate. And this hook on my arm isn't meant to rip you to shreds. No indeed. I'm saving that honor for a lad named Peter Pan. That is, if the proper authorities don't nab him before I do.

Although Peter Pan knows nothing about honor, I certainly do. I was brought up to be a proper gentleman. I learned manners, ethics, and values from my parents and at school. Ah, school. What fond memories I have from my days at school! There I gained my sense of duty and of responsibility. I learned everything I needed to know in order to be a useful member of society. Those valuable lessons are exactly what that lad Peter Pan has missed. He should go to school! And he should grow up and take his proper place in society, whatever that may be. It wouldn't matter how he served his community— he could be anything from a chimney sweep to a judge. One simply must contribute in some way.

How do I, Captain Hook, contribute? Well, mate, have a seat and let me tell you my tale. Would you like a spot of tea before I begin?

I got my start in the shipping business some years back. With funds from my family, I purchased a lovely ship named the Jolly Roger. I know I have been very fortunate in life, and I never neglect my responsibility to aid those who have been less fortunate. So when it was time to hire a crew, I looked for mates who were doing poorly. I offered them a very pleasant life at sea with good financial rewards in exchange for their hard work. Many were grateful for such a chance and accepted my job offer in an instant.

We began sailing at once and transported goods from one country to another. We enjoyed many successful voyages. Of course, as captain, I stressed the importance of hard work from the very start. And, being a good leader, I involved the crew in governing the ship. Together we wrote a list of shipboard rules and a code of punishment for those who broke the rules. I'm glad to say that we never had to use that code. (Although I admit that once we got dangerously close to doing so.) To enforce the rules, I relied mainly on the rewards for a job well done. I was very generous in letting the crew share in the profits.

The crew responded well to these conditions. They respected me and grew to respect themselves, too. A person simply cannot respect himself as a ne'er-do-well. Without self respect, a person has little. I gave these men their sense of worth by giving them duties to perform and responsibilities to carry out. To boot, I promised rewards for jobs well done. We collected huge chests of gold for our toils.

And one would simply not believe the opportunity for adventure on the open sea! When all the work was done, my crew and I had a fine time. Sometimes we visited other ships. Other times we went ashore to seaboard towns. Every place we went, people knew us and granted our every wish.

In the course of our travels, we discovered this wonderful, little island. We decided to use it as our home port. Each time we completed a voyage, we returned to the island to prepare for our next journey.

One day, as the mates and I were making some minor repairs to the ship, we saw something very odd.

It was Laughing Eddy who halted our work by saying, "Now that's what I call strange!"

"Aye, now what is this all about?" I asked. Then I looked up and saw what had attracted his attention. "I say, mates, it appears to be a bird shaped like a boy."

"That's no bird flapping its wings!" said my bosun Smee. "That's a boy who can fly. You don't see many of them nowadays, do you?"

"A boy who can fly? We could use one of those on our crew," I said, always ready to offer a lad an opportunity. "He could fly over the water and alert us of any trouble ahead." In spite of the fine life we enjoyed, the high seas could be a dangerous place. Some chaps in this business did not conduct themselves with the same kind of courtesy we offered.

The mates and I watched the boy land in a tree. I ambled over and called up to him. "Hello, up there! How would you like a job? You seem to have quite a talent for flying. You could be a scout for my ship. The job pays well and offers a great future in exchange for your hard work. What do you think, lad?"

Then the boy looked down at me and spoke in an extremely rude manner. "My name is Peter Pan. I ran away from home on the day I was born because I overheard my mother and father planning to put me to work some day. You see, I don't plan to grow up. I intend to remain a boy forever and always have fun."

I was shocked by that lad's attitude and words. What he said went against everything I had been brought up to believe. It also opposed everything we had worked to achieve on the Jolly Roger.

"Shhhhhh!" I said. "My mates certainly don't need to hear any talk like that. If you don't plan to work with my crew, then you need to leave this island before my mates start taking on any of your ideas."

Pan said, "I don't plan to work for you or for anyone else. And I won't leave this island either. This island is my Neverland and this is where I plan to play for the rest of my life. Isn't that right, Tinker Bell?" Then I noticed this tiny fairy girl who had a light shining from within her.

She stopped flitting around long enough to say, "That's right, Peter, and if that ugly pirate doesn't like it, he can leave the island." Then Tinker Bell shone her bright light directly into my eyes. Pan then flew into the air and shouted, "I'm youth! I'm joy! I'm the little bird that has broken out of the egg!"

I didn't know which puzzled me more—being called a "pirate" (I don't think of myself as a pirate, but more of a trade expert) or Peter Pan's ridiculous statements.

But with a hateful attitude like that, I knew that Pan would present a problem. At first, I thought there was some hope for him and his friend Tinker Bell. In an effort to redirect the mistaken youths, I had my bosun Smee direct messages to them. When they flew near the ship, Smee shouted at them. "GET A JOB! YOU'LL BE HAPPIER WHEN YOU'RE WORKING!" I had the mates print signs and post them all over Neverland.

Time went on this way. We tried to convince Pan that he needed a job, but he wouldn't hear of it. He just flitted around the island all the day long.

Then six more boys came to live on the island. Pan put out some ridiculous story that they were "lost boys" who had fallen from their carriages and were sent to him. Apparently, he appointed himself captain of these boys. That certainly annoyed me. The position of captain is an honorable one that should be earned. Besides, I suspected foul play on the part of Peter Pan. I believed that he had kidnapped those boys and left grieving parents behind.

Because we called the island our home port, I felt a responsibility to look after the safety of those who lived there. If the boys had indeed been kidnapped, I would see that they were returned to their parents.

I found the boys exploring the shore and admiring the ship. As always, I began by offering them an opportunity. "Hello, mates," I said. "We need a couple of hard working cabin boys and a few good mates to swab the deck as well. The pay is fair, but you must be willing to work hard," I told them. I wanted them to know what they were getting into. This is no job for people who are unwilling to work.

They said, "Captain Peter doesn't want us to work."

I could see that Pan had already ruined this lot. "Is that right?" I asked. "What does your captain want you to do?"

"He wants us to play, just like he does," they said.

"I see. How will you survive? How will you pay your way?" I asked. "What about duty, responsibility, and the need to contribute to society?"

The boys answered me with blank stares. I could tell that Peter Pan had impressed his own misguided notions on the lads. The boys seemed to know nothing about proper values. I tried another subject, perhaps one they could discuss intelligently.

"Do you like it here? Are you being held against your will?" I asked.

"We love Neverland! We love Captain Peter!" they shouted and scampered back the way they had come.

I went back aboard ship. Thoughts of those boys bothered me. I feared that those troubled youths might turn to a life of crime in order to survive. And if they did turn to a life of crime, we and the other citizens of the island would be their victims. My men and I had worked years to acquire our wealth, and we had no plans to part with it.

I knew I had to try again to reform Pan. I made my way to the island. I hadn't been there long when I spotted him. "Hello," I began. "How are things on the island?"

"In Neverland, you mean," Pan answered rudely.

"Ah, yes, your Neverland," I agreed in order to hold his attention. "Well, I'm here as the captain of my ship to tell you that because this is our port, I am also the captain of Neverland. And because I am a true captain, you must obey my orders. Either you work aboard my ship, or you and the other boys must leave the island."

"Is that so?" said Pan, reaching for his sword.

"Aye, that's so," I said and reached for my sword as well. Of course, I never intended to fight him. I just wanted to show him who was in charge. I couldn't have him thinking that I was afraid of a flying boy and his tiny, flying friend, could I? But, as I said, I never planned to fight Pan. I only wanted him to respect me. After I earned his respect, I felt I could reform him, just as I had done with my crew.

I knew Pan was lazy, but I had no idea he was vicious. I had drawn my sword only as a show of power. He, on the other hand, had *every* intention of harming me. When he lunged at me, I couldn't believe it!

I had no choice but to fight back. I tried to defend myself without hurting the boy, but the fight turned mean. Of course, I fought by the rules of fairness that I had been taught since childhood. But I soon realized that Peter Pan was not a fair person. He was a criminally-minded child! I've been in some sinister fights in my day, but I had never had a fight like that one. The lad was flying as he was fighting! First he was over my head. Then, in a flash, he was behind me. "Where is the rascal?" I yelled. Finally, I got him by the throat and held my blade against his neck. I thought perhaps I could frighten some sense into him. But before I could say anything, that Tinker Bell flew into my eyes and blinded me with her glaring light! How unfair! That is no way to fight! I didn't have a chance with that wicked fairy blinding me.

As I staggered around trying to regain my sight, Pan took advantage of the situation. With one swish of his sword, my arm was gone. I was in terrible pain, as you can imagine. A part of my body had been lopped off, after all. But being a gentleman, I bore the pain with dignity. My sight returned just in time for me to see Pan fling my arm to the jaws of a waiting crocodile.

That croc swallowed my arm in one gulp. Then, pleased with the taste, the huge beast licked its lips and opened its jaws for the rest of me. I got out of there fast! Aye, you can depend on that! But that wasn't the end of Pan's evil deed. You see, that croc took a special liking to the way I tasted. It started to follow me around to get the rest of me. One night I woke up in my bed to see the beast's jaws about to clamp down on me. I grabbed the closest thing at hand, a clock, and threw it into those gaping jaws. Then I ran away from the huge beast.

From that point on, whenever that croc was in the vicinity, I would hear *tick tick* coming from the clock in its belly. Aye, I would get out of there before one could say, "That croc likes the taste of the captain."

"You might say that's a compliment to you, Captain," my bosun Smee was fond of pointing out. "That croc has jaws only for you."

"I don't need any such compliments," I replied to Smee. "What I need is a replacement for my missing arm." And I got one—an iron hook. After I became used to it, I actually found the hook to be quite useful. Of course, it did remind me of that hateful Peter Pan.

I adjusted well to my injury, but I knew that not everyone is as forgiving as I am. I felt that Peter Pan should not be allowed to maim anyone else. Neither should he be allowed to further damage those miserable lost boys. I set out to stop Peter Pan.

Smee and I searched the island. I found a toadstool that immediately looked suspicious to me. Upon closer examination, we saw it was a chimney. Aye, we had found Pan's underground hideout! Smee put his ear to the ground and overheard the boys talking. Pan wasn't there, but they said he was out looking for some new recruits. He especially wanted a mother for the boys.

Just as Smee and I were planning the best way to capture the lost boys, we heard *tick tick*. Smee and I fled for the safety of the ship.

Now that we knew where they lived, my mates and I could study the comings and goings of that little group of wrongdoers. Soon their crew grew larger. They were preparing themselves for more mischief. The six boys had turned into eight. And there was this young mother, too. Aye, she was brought in to train the young ones in the corrupt ways of Peter Pan.

Something had to be done. So one day, my mates and I waited outside their underground home. As the boys came up, we nabbed them. We gagged them so they couldn't cry out to warn that sinister Pan. Then we bound each lad so he couldn't fly away. We got all the boys and that mother of theirs named Wendy.

"Take them to the Jolly Roger," I said to my men.

"I'll take care of Pan myself."

The plan was to ship all the children back to London. That was probably where Pan had kidnapped them. The children would fare well once they returned to their homes.

I lowered myself into the underground house quietly. And then I located Pan, who was asleep on his bed. It would have been so easy to plunge my dagger into the scheming lad's heart. But, I had no cause to harm him—I just wanted him off the island. To do that, I had to get him on a ship. If he stayed asleep, he would be no problem. So I just put a few drops of a sleeping potion in the lad's medicine.

Then I silently crawled from the underground house and returned to the Jolly Roger. Before I brought Pan aboard, I wanted to try to undo some of the damage he had caused to the boys and their young mother. Without Peter Pan's evil presence, I might be able to improve the children's attitude toward work. When we finally brought Pan on the ship, we would isolate him so he could do no more damage to the children.

To test the extent of Pan's influence, I said, "Six of you lads will walk the plank, but I have space aboard for two cabin boys. Who wants the job?"

I assumed that two would take the offer. I would then send those two lads away and say, "Four of you lads will walk the plank, but I have space aboard for two deck boys. Who wants the job?" When there were only two boys left, I planned to make them step up on the plank. Before they walked into the ocean, I'd offer them another chance at a job. I thought by then they would be ready to work. In that way, I hoped to undo some of the evil influence of Peter Pan.

But Pan had left his mark. Not one said, "I'll take the job." Those lads chose certain death rather than accepting a job.

Aye, I became desperate. It seemed that those boys would not work, no matter what. "Bring up the girl," I called. "Make her face the sight of her young ones walking the plank." Maybe the mother would encourage her young ones to take a job if the other choice was death. I counted on Wendy to scream, "No matter what Peter Pan says, work is not that bad! Take the job!"

But I never spoke with the girl. Instead, I heard that most fearsome of all sounds—*tick tick*. I would be a tasty morsel for the croc if I didn't make a hasty exit.

My loyal crew took me to safety, and then something strange happened. We heard my quartermaster's death cry, followed by a rooster crowing "doodle-doo!"

"What was that?" we all asked. Then we heard the crowing again. "Doodle-doo!"

I am proud to say that I was a courageous captain in the midst of danger. So that I would be alive to sink with my ship if necessary, I ordered one mate after another into the cabin to battle this unknown monster. One after another, we heard their death screams followed by the "doodle-doo!"

At last I had no choice. I took up the lantern and entered the cabin. The next thing I knew the lantern was yanked from my hand and some strange thing crowed "doodle-doo" in my ear. I left the cabin in a hurry.

Then I had a brainstorm. We would let the lost boys battle the "doodle-doo." After they finished I would explain that they had done a job. Then I could praise them for a job well done. I would even pay them a small wage for their task. I thought that might encourage them to get steady work and turn their back on the lazy habits they had learned from Peter Pan. So we shoved one lad into the cabin and waited. We heard nothing. Then, one at a time, we shoved the rest of them in. Finally we heard something—a giant "doodle-doo!" This one was louder than all the others.

My men tried to jump ship. "There's a monster aboard!" they cried. I did my best to calm them, only to discover too late the real cause of our problems. Aye, it was a monster indeed—Peter Pan! No wonder none of those boys had accepted my offers of work. They had a better plan for making their way in life—murder my mates and me and steal our gold.

Pan and the boys burst from the cabin and attacked us. My men were so startled by Pan's trickery that their fighting was pitiful. I tried to stand off Pan and his lads by myself. "Proud and sinister youth, prepare to meet your doom!" I cried, and the fighting began.

I was as brave as any man could be in the face of all that danger. There were so many of them—Pan, all those boys, and that pesky, little Tinker Bell!

As I swung my sword against this attack, Tinker Bell flashed her light into my eyes again. She blinded me! I couldn't see at all. I stumbled and fell overboard.

My sight returned just as I neared the water. Then I saw my nightmare come true! The jaws of that wicked crocodile were waiting for me. I heard no *tick tick*. Where was my warning? And then I realized—the clock inside the croc had finally stopped running.

I screamed in agony. At that moment I wished I could fly like Pan! The croc got my leg, but not the rest of me.

So now Peter Pan has cost me an arm and a leg! Because of him, I have a hook for an arm and a peg for a leg. Aye, a peg with a dagger in it to use the next time Pan and I meet. Then I'll act like no gentleman. I'll fight like that rogue Peter Pan.

So, I wait for Pan. In the meantime I fill my days with painting, reading, and gardening. I just completed the most delightful little landscape. And I read everything I can get my hand and hook on. I prefer Chaucer, Shakespeare—really any fine literature. And my flowers do bring me such happiness. My tea roses are simply outstanding this year!

I would prefer to take care of Pan myself. But of course, I recognize that if the proper authorities seize him before I do, justice will still be served. In fact, there would be a certain satisfaction in knowing that Pan was imprisoned. He certainly has committed criminal acts. I truly believe he kidnapped those children. And surely there is a law that forbids turning children against work. I fear for the safety of others—adults and children alike—as long as Pan remains free.

Prison would be a good place for Pan. He'd be forced to work every day, and perhaps he would even receive some formal schooling. Aye, that's all I ever wanted— for Peter Pan to grow up and get a job.

Steck-Vaughn

POINT
of
VIEW
Stories

Peter Pan

A Classic Tale

Written by

J.M. Barrie

Retold by

Dr. Alvin Granowsky

Illustrated by

Judith Cheng

RSVP

RAINTREE
STECK-VAUGHN
P U B L I S H E R S
The Steck-Vaughn Company

Austin, Texas

Long ago in London, there lived a family called the Darlings. Mr. and Mrs. Darling had three children—Wendy, the oldest, then John, then little Michael. The family was quite ordinary, except in one respect. They employed a dog as a nanny. The family had found the dog one day on a stroll through Kensington Gardens and named her Nana.

Mrs. Darling thought Nana was a wonderful nursemaid. The gentle dog took exceptional care of the children. Mr. Darling was pleased as well, although he was a bit afraid other folks might think it odd for them to have a dog as a nanny. The Darlings were a simple, happy family until one very strange night.

If Mr. and Mrs. Darling had known what was going to happen that evening, they never would have left the house. And even though Mr. Darling was angry with Nana, he never would have chained her outside away from the children. But they did both of those things, and so they allowed the children to have a great adventure.

It was dark in the nursery as the children slept. A young boy and a tiny fairy girl opened the window and flew inside. "Fly away with me to Neverland!" said the boy.

Wendy opened her eyes and thought she was dreaming. "I say, there's a boy in the nursery!" she said. John and Michael woke up at the sound of her exclamation.

"What is your name?" the boy asked.

"Wendy Moira Angela Darling," she replied. "And these are my brothers, John and Michael. What is your name?"

"Peter Pan," the boy answered. "And this is Tinker Bell." When Tink talked, the children heard only the delicate tinkling of bells. Only Peter understood what she said.

Then Wendy asked where the visitors lived, and Peter explained to her about Neverland. "Neverland is a place for lost boys," said Peter. "They are the boys who fell out of their carriages when their nursemaids weren't looking. When nobody claimed them after seven days, they were sent to me in Neverland. I am their captain."

"How did you get to be the captain?" Wendy asked. "Did you fall out of your carriage first?"

"Of course not," said Peter. "I ran away from home on the very day I was born. I heard Mother and Father planning what I was to be when I grew up. I never want to grow up—I'd much rather be a boy all my life and have fun."

"Wendy, if you come with me to Neverland, you can be a mother for the lost boys," Peter said. "You see, they have no one to tell them bedtime stories. I'll bet you can tell an excellent bedtime story."

Wendy did think all children deserved a very nice bedtime story, but she wasn't sure it was a good idea to leave her wonderful home and loving parents.

"How might I get to Neverland?" Wendy asked.

"We'll fly!" said Peter.

"I don't know how to fly," said Wendy in her most grown-up voice.

"I will teach you!" exclaimed Peter proudly.

"I say, Peter," John asked, "can you actually fly?"

Peter smiled and flew to the ceiling.

"That's a fine trick!" said John. "How do you do it?"

"You just think happy thoughts, and they lift you up into the air," Peter said. Then he demonstrated for them again.

But no matter how many happy thoughts, the children could not fly. They jumped from their beds high in the air and came down with a thunderous thud.

Then Peter remembered that no one can fly without fairy dust. He just happened to have a handful and blew some on each of the children. "Now fly!" he said.

Michael went first and in an instant flew across the room. Then John and Wendy did the same. Soon the children were flying all about the nursery.

"It's time to leave for Neverland!" Peter laughed, knowing he had captured the children's fancy.

"It will be an adventure!" cried John. That is exactly what Peter had been planning. Michael and John were anxious to leave, especially since Peter had whispered in their ear, "There are pirates in Neverland." Peter waved for the children to follow him through the window.

"Hurry!" he called. "Neverland is second to the right and straight on to morning!"

The children didn't exactly understand Peter's directions, but he and Tink stayed close to show them the way. After flying for some time, Peter announced, "We're here!"

"Where is here?" the children wanted to know.

"See where the arrows are pointing?" asked Peter.

The children took another look into the night sky and did indeed see hundreds of twinkling arrows pointing to an island.

The children sensed something fearsome in the air and drew closer to Peter. Their progress had become labored as if something warned them not to continue. Peter's eyes gleamed with excitement. "They don't want us to land," he said, without explaining who they might be.

"Are you open to adventure?" Peter asked. "There's a pirate sleeping below us. We can kill him if you'd like."

"But what if he wakes up first?" asked John nervously.

Peter was shocked. "You don't imagine I would kill him while he was asleep, do you? How cowardly that would be! First I would awaken him. That's the way I like to do it."

"I say, do you kill many?" John asked, properly impressed.

"Boatloads of them," Peter boasted. "That's one of the reasons their captain is out to get me."

"Who is their captain?" asked John.

"Hook!" answered Peter grimly.

Both boys gasped. "Not James Hook!" they said in unison.

"Aye," answered Peter, looking even more stern.

Then Michael, who in truth was just a very little boy, began to cry, and John took several deep gulps of air. They knew that Hook was the most terrible of all the pirates. John trembled at the thought of Captain Hook. He knew Hook was once the bosun to the fierce pirate Blackbeard. Together the two had terrorized everyone on the high seas.

"Is he as bad as they say? Is he very big?" asked John.

"No," said Peter, "he is not as bad as they say. He is even worse. But, fortunately, he is not as big as he used to be. You see, I cut off a part of him."

"You cut off a part of him!" John and Michael's eyes were wide from excitement. "What part?"

"His right arm," said Peter. "He's replaced the arm with an iron hook. He uses his hook as a claw. He tears mates to bits with that hook."

Then Peter added, "There is one thing that every boy who serves under me has to promise."

John grew pale, "Yes?"

"If it comes to an open fight between Hook and me, you must not join in the fight. It is most important that I finish off Hook by myself. Will you promise?" Peter asked.

"Yes, you can depend on that," John said quickly.

For a moment, things seemed a bit lighter. Tink was flying near Peter and the children with her light shining brightly. Then suddenly, there came a tremendous crash. The pirates had fired their cannon, Long Tom, directly at them. No one was hit, but the blast gave each of the Darling children a fright.

The island seemed to come alive with anticipation of Peter's return. The pirates had grown restless. They sang gleefully, knowing that the time for action would be very soon. The six boys who served under Peter felt the tension. They heard the pirates' song and hid in their underground home, awaiting their fearless leader.

The treacherous captain of the pirates spoke to his faithful bosun Smee. "Most of all," Hook said as he sat down upon a huge toadstool, "I want their captain, Peter Pan. 'Twas he who cut off my arm." He waved his hook in a most frightening way. "I'll tear him to bits with this!" Hook said fiercely.

The captain shuddered as he remembered the day that young Pan sliced off his arm and flung it to a crocodile that happened by. That croc developed a taste for the pirate. It liked his arm so much that the croc, licking its lips and waiting for the rest of him, had followed Hook from that day forward. Lucky for Captain Hook, the crocodile had also swallowed a clock. Its *tick tick* warned the pirate away from the dangers of the crocodile's jaws. However, the warning would not last forever. Hook knew that one day the clock would wind down.

Hook jumped up. "This toadstool is hot!" Then he examined the mushroom and found that it was actually a chimney. He had discovered the boys' underground home! Smee pressed his ear to the ground and listened to the boys talking. "Peter Pan's still away," he whispered.

"Aye, we'll be ready for his return," said Hook. "Let's go back to the ship and prepare a cake for the lost boys—a cake cooked with green sugar. Since the boys have no mother, they will not know how dangerous it is to eat rich, damp cake. They will eat it and then they will die!"

Before the two nasty pirates could begin their sinister plan, they heard a noise. *Tick tick*. The sound was unmistakable. *Tick tick*. Hook shuddered and said, "The crocodile!" He dashed off with Smee close behind.

Finally, Peter and the children landed on the island. Peter showed them the way to the underground house and introduced them to the lost boys. In the days that followed, the Darling children grew to love that underground house almost as much as their own. Wendy took over as the mother to the lost boys. She cooked, cleaned, mended clothes, and felt very happy and needed. Did she miss her own loving mother and father? Now and then, but she didn't really worry. She knew they would always leave the window open for John, Michael, and her.

When Peter was home, he would help a bit with the children. But he did not enjoy pretending to be their father. "This is only make-believe, I trust? You know I am too young to be a father," he would say.

After dinner, Wendy would tell a good-night story. She would settle the boys all around her. Sometimes she would tell a fairy tale. Other times she would tell a story the boys loved—a story Peter did not like one bit. "There was once a happy couple named Mr. and Mrs. Darling who had three lovely children. Now the children had a wonderful nursemaid named Nana. One day Mr. Darling became angry at Nana and chained her up in the yard. On that very night, the children met an unusual boy, and they all flew away to Neverland."

"Does this story have a sad ending?" asked a lost boy.

"No indeed," replied Wendy. She was now approaching the part that Peter disliked most. Often, he would leave the room so he wouldn't have to hear the story's ending, but this night he remained. "The Darling children knew that their mother would always leave the window open for them to fly home. So they stayed away for years and had a wonderful time. When they returned, the window was open, just as it had been on the night they departed. So they flew to their mother and father, and everyone was happy."

Peter groaned. "Wendy," he said, "you are wrong about mothers. Years ago I thought my mother would keep the window open for me. But when I flew back, the window was locked, and another little boy was sleeping in my bed."

"Wendy, let's go home now!" John and Michael cried.

Wendy hugged her brothers close to her. "Peter, please do what is necessary for our return. Immediately!"

The lost boys became terribly upset at the thought of losing Wendy. But when she saw their unhappiness, she exclaimed, "You may all come home with me. I am sure Mother and Father will adopt you!"

The boys cried out happily, "Peter, can we go? Can we?"

"If that's what you want," said Peter. He was devastated at the thought of losing Wendy and the boys, but he would never let it show. "Of course, I shall not come with you."

The boys quickly packed their belongings.

"No tears or other foolishness," said Peter. He acted as if he weren't upset at all. He turned to Tink. "You will be their guide. Good-bye, all!" Then Peter turned away.

But right overhead, the pirates were back. They had set up a vigilant watch for Peter and the boys.

One of the lost boys climbed out of the underground house. He rose right into the arms of Smee. Smee tossed him to another pirate, who then tossed him to yet another. Every boy received the same rough treatment. They were thrown down the line like bales of hay. When Wendy climbed out last, she was not treated so poorly. Hook bowed graciously to her and smiled with false politeness. He grandly offered Wendy his hook and escorted her to the spot where the boys were gagged and tied, unable to cry out or fly away.

Tink, who had flown to the safety of a treetop, watched the treacherous scene unfold.

Hook motioned to his men to take Wendy and the boys to their ship. "I want to take care of that insolent Peter Pan myself," Hook said menacingly.

When Hook was alone, he listened for a moment. Was Pan asleep or was he waiting with a dagger? There was no way to tell. Silently, he lowered himself into the darkened room. As his eyes grew accustomed to the dim light below, Hook made out the form of Peter asleep on the bed.

Peter, unaware of the tragedy going on above ground, laid on his bed to grieve over the loss of Wendy and the boys. He nearly cried, but forced himself to laugh instead. Finally, he had fallen asleep.

Hook stood over the sleeping boy and considered the best way to do him in. Hook thought, "He must suffer as much as possible." Then he saw the medicine that Wendy had left out for Peter. Hook formed a plan. He took a dreadful poison from his pouch and added five big drops of it to Peter's medicine. Then Hook silently climbed back up above ground.

Peter slept on. Suddenly he was awakened by a tap at the door. Peter felt for his dagger and then asked, "Who is it?"

"Peter, let me in!" cried Tink. He cracked open the door, and she flew in excitedly. Quickly, she blurted out the horrible tale about the capture of Wendy and the boys.

"I'll rescue them!" Peter exclaimed. He leapt up to find his weapons. Before departing, he thought of something he could do to please Wendy. "I'll take my medicine!" he thought. His hand closed around the deadly liquid.

"No!" shrieked Tinker Bell. "Don't take that medicine!" She had heard Hook laughing about the poison. As Peter raised the medicine to his mouth, Tink darted in front of him. She drank down the medicine to the very last drop.

"Hook poisoned your medicine, Peter," said Tinker Bell in a weak voice. "Soon I will die."

"Did you drink it to save me?" asked Peter.

"Yes," said Tinker Bell. Tink's light grew faint as the poison took effect. Tink tried to tell Peter something, but her voice was so quiet that he could barely make out the message. Finally, he understood her to say that she thought she might get well if only children believed in fairies.

But there were no children present. So Peter called out to children dreaming of Neverland, "If you believe in fairies, clap your hands! Don't let Tinker Bell die!"

Many children must have clapped, for Tink grew stronger in less than a minute. Soon she was flitting about the room.

"Now to save Wendy and the boys," Peter said as he set out on his perilous quest.

Back on the Jolly Roger, Hook marched around the deck triumphantly. He thought Peter was done in, and the other boys were about to walk the plank. Hook said to the boys, "Some of you will walk the plank, but I have space aboard for two cabin boys. Which of you shall it be?"

Their legs trembled as they looked at the short plank. Still, every one refused Hook's offer.

"Your fate is sealed!" cried Hook. "The young mother will watch her children walk the plank." Just then the *tick tick* of the crocodile stopped Hook in his tracks.

An amazing change crept over the once so fierce captain. He crumbled into a heap. "Hide me!" he begged.

As the pirates took Hook away, the captives rushed to the side of the ship to see what had saved them. But it was no croc coming to their aid. It was Peter!

Peter laughed to see the pirates retreating. His crocodile act had tricked the whole lot of them.

Peter had to work quickly to save Wendy and the boys. With a deep strike from his dagger, he finished off the quartermaster and hurried to the ship's cabin. Then Peter hid in the cabin where he crowed like a rooster. Hook shouted orders and waved his hook, forcing one terrified pirate after another into that cabin to fight the monster. Peter defended himself and battled the pirates one by one. Soon Wendy and the boys would be free.

"The ship is haunted!" screamed the superstitious pirates. Now they were more afraid of the terrible spirit in the cabin than the vicious hook on their leader's arm.

Hook seized a lantern and ran into the cabin. "I'll finish off that doodle-doo myself!" he screamed.

But a moment later, he staggered from the cabin fearful and shaken. "Something blew out the light," he gasped.

The men cried, "The ship is doomed! We will all die!"

Then Hook had an idea. "Drive in the boys," he ordered. "Let them fight that doodle-doo! They might kill it. If it kills them, we're best rid of them."

As the pirates shoved them into the cabin, the boys cried out, pretending to be afraid.

Inside the cabin, Peter quickly undid the boys' shackles and armed them with what weapons they could find. Then he gave a giant crow as a signal to the pirates that the boys were dead.

Pandemonium broke loose. "Lads," cried Hook, "I've thought it out. Bad luck's aboard."

"It's you!" they screamed. "The man with a hook!"

"No!" cried Hook. "Women aboard ship bring bad luck. Throw the girl overboard!"

The pirates charged at Wendy. "No one can save you from a watery grave!" they cried.

"Peter Pan can!" replied Peter as he burst from the cabin. Peter took control as the pirates stood by in shock. "Charge them!" he commanded the boys, and the free-for-all began. Peter was everywhere, his dagger flashing to and fro. At last, only Peter and Captain Hook remained. "It's you or me this time!" cried Peter as he dashed at Captain Hook.

"Foolish youth!" mocked Hook. "Prepare to meet your doom!"

"Evil old man!" replied Peter. "Prepare to die! I'm youth! I'm joy! I'm the little bird that has broken out of the egg!"

The fighting was fierce, but Hook proved no match for Peter. Hook saw no hope of winning the fight and leapt into the sea. He did not know that the crocodile lay waiting for him in the water below. As he had long feared, the clock inside the croc had finally stopped ticking. Thus ended the life of the terrible pirate James Hook. Wendy, her brothers, and the lost boys were all saved!

Back in the Darling home, Mrs. Darling spoke to the nursemaid. "Oh, Nana, I dreamt my dear ones had come home," she said.

"Please shut the nursery window, dearest," Mr. Darling asked his wife. "I feel a draft coming from that room."

"Oh, George, the window must always be left open for the children's return!" said Mrs. Darling. "Please, never shut that window!"

That very night, the children quietly returned. Peter Pan arrived first and planned to ask Tink to shut the window. "When Wendy comes, she'll think her mother shut her out. Then she will go back to Neverland with me and stay there forever."

But when Peter looked in the window, he saw Mrs. Darling. He realized that she missed her children dreadfully, so he left the window open. Wendy, John, and Michael flew to their beds and slipped under the covers.

One more time Mrs. Darling checked the nursery, but this time all the beds were occupied. Her children had returned! Mrs. Darling called for her husband to share her joy. What a happy scene when Mr. Darling and Nana also saw the children in the nursery!

The lost boys waited downstairs while Wendy told their incredible story to her parents. Mrs. Darling said at once, "They can be part of our family!" Mr. Darling thought six was a rather large number, but somehow it all worked out.

Then Mrs. Darling saw Peter. "Since we're adopting the other boys, why don't we adopt you, too?"

"Will I go to school?" asked Peter. "And later on, will you expect me to find a job?"

"I imagine so," said Mrs. Darling. "That is a common thing to do."

"Not for me it isn't!" replied Peter. "I don't want to go to school. I don't want to spend my life working. I want to be a boy forever and always have fun!"

"But where will you live?" asked Mrs. Darling.

"In the underground house with Tink," said Peter.

"Won't it be lonely there?" asked Wendy.

Mrs. Darling noticed the sad twitch on Peter's lips and made him a generous offer. "Wendy can join you for one week each year to help you with your spring cleaning," she said.

This promise made Peter very happy, and he started to fly about the room. When he reached the window Wendy called to him, "Please, don't forget me!"

"Never!" promised Peter as he flew away.

And for a while, he did not forget Wendy. For a couple of years he came for her in the springtime. They had a wonderful time in Neverland cleaning the underground house. Then several springs passed and he came no more. Eventually Wendy forgot Peter. Actually, as she got older she began to wonder whether he really existed at all. For you see, as Wendy found out, all children grow up— except for one.